Winner of the 27th Annual International 3-Day Novel Contest

love block

**meghan austin &
shannon mullally**

3-day books
vancouver   toronto

3-Day Books
341 Water Street, Suite 200
Vancouver, B.C., V6B 1B8
Canada

Printed and bound in Canada
Cover art ı Jeremy Bruneel
Design ı Bibelot Communications
Edited by ı Nicole Marteinsson

Library and Archives Canada Cataloguing in Publication
Austin, Meghan, 1979-
Mullally, Shannon, 1978-

Love Block
Meghan Austin and Shannon Mullally

"Winner of the 27th Annual International 3-Day Novel Contest"

ISBN-13 : 978-155152-194-7.--
ISBN-10: 1-55152-194-6

I. Title
PS3601.U76L69   2005   813'.6   C2005-902626-X

Distributed in Canada and the United States by Arsenal Pulp Press

acknowledgements

The authors would like to thank Lorraine Affourtit, Stephen Hawking, Franz Kafka, Clarice Lispector and Marguerite Yourcenar for their words.

The authors thank Melissa Edwards and Barbara Zatyko for their special kind of possibility.

Agent 160:

Enclosed, please find the following requested items:

1. rope

2. personal lubricant (pump top)

I assume—from the contents of today's shipment—
that you are making progress, as they say.

I was unable to locate the following item(s):

___love block____

Is this a topical solution? Please advise.~Agent K.

Agent K:

Did I not tell you? The solution is never topical. If I were a different

angle, I would be sad. Continue. I have enclosed what you asked of me.

Sometimes, the zipper sticks.

—160

160:

I appreciate the gesture, but this is not what I requested at all. This is not a new life. This is a body bag. ~AK

160:

Forgive me if my last letter was abrupt. I've been in a strange mood, a side effect of Plan B (pills). I've got three prescriptions going. Two of these a day and you'll never feel like contact with any human ever again. I eat them like cough drops. Only the cherry flavour is available. I hear there is also an orange. ~AK

Agent K:

I sent you the wrong package. The one with the prairie in it went to heaven.

Now, is abrupt.

—160

Agent K:

This city is a pair of dirty trousers. The regulations are for us. I fear I am off track. I unwrapped the rope and the lube. If it stopped raining today, something would happen. The streets are short enough.

—130+30

160:
Today, at the doctor's office, I saw a woman who looked just like Jeannette, that French maid I used to see. If I'm not mistaken, you saw her as well a few times. Or she saw you. You're not off track. I just received the reports, haven't had a chance to look them over.

Let's make sure these records get destroyed. I'm going to smoke a cigarette, then let's figure out what to do with the body.

Did I say body? I meant: BOY.
~AK

K:

I only forgive those with a fixed mouth. The orange ones screw with my stomach. The cherry ones sound nice. Be sure to send some with your next shipment. Don't be late. Is someone counting on something?

—160

160:
In August of 1997, Jeannette suffered the first of a series of hallucinations that she would spend our time together obsessively documenting and re-documenting.

"The problem," Jeannette writes in one of her early notebooks, "is not that I don't remember what happened, but that what happened did not happen in words. I have no memories."

Her symptoms: nausea, loss of consciousness, auditory hallucinations, *jamais vois* (I had to look this up:

the contrary of *déjà vu*), all were consistent with epilepsy, specifically temporal lobe, Jeannette concluded, December 1999. She never mentioned this diagnosis to me or anyone else. She told me she feared she was losing her sanity. I bought her a typewriter.
~K

Agent K:

Jeannette? I will admit that she saw me. It was an embarrassment. If I had been an amateur, she would have lifted my hat and left my skirt.

—Junior 160

160:
Jeannette admitted she was seeing many people. She didn't believe in monogamy. At one point, she was seeing (professionally) three therapists. The two women found out about each other; she dropped the man because his solution for every-thing was: "Stop smoking so much dope."
~K

Dear Gravity (Agent K):

I have read about Simone's death. It is the same as her life. Is that a comfort?

I just listened to Pigeon's message four times. His question is laughable. The danger is in my repetition.

It is late here. It is always late here. Are you watching?

—Grace (160)

> I'm watching. He just keeps coming back. Have you
> tipped him?
> ~K

Agent K:

This was discovered in the tape deck of my newly (acquired) powder-blue Buick.

A Dr. L is speaking:

Patient 137 took offense to my well-advised advice that I gave her for her many inappropriate "affairs" as we have agreed to call them (a neutral, woman-friendly term). Or the most offensive. At any rate, I told her to quit "smoking dope." She threw a typewriter at my head. I called her crazy. It was a typical session with no reason to suspect her of displaying rational thought anytime in the near future.

Mental note: Should I be sleeping with her?

Agent K:

Another boy lost his money. He looked at me and saw gold. What did I see? A neighbourhood above my neighbourhood. Out of all the metals, beryllium is my favourite. Now you know something that is not reported.

In 1997, I made her too many sandwiches. If you look carefully into her notebooks you will see the crumbs. If you do not see them, I will argue your clumsiness.

—Gretal (160)

160:
Summer is over, agent. I know you don't cook. And Jeannette doesn't eat. Let's put that in the past tense. The boys are multiplying. And where is my girl (not the French maid, but **xxxx**)? Will **xxxx** be here soon?
~K

Agent K:

Does **xxxx** know? If she does not know anything, she will not come. If she knows something she will still not come. If she knows everything . . . who can know everything? She may come. If you gave her directions, she will have to lose them. I think that is important. It probably isn't that important. Perhaps the love block is imported. Will you check your international contacts?

Marguerite Yourcenar said love is a punishment for not being able to be alone. This time, I am inclined to agree.

I met a baby last night. She was not my baby. She was the daughter of a poet so she sleeps well. The last time I slept well, someone had knocked me unconscious.

Do we have an arch-nemesis?

—Agent 160

160:
Everyone knows, which is why **xxxx** doesn't. No pressure to move the information along. My doctor said that love as generic disease already has an international spokesperson. "Better cancer," he said, "better..." and he brought out a chart of the "fifty top and most recent diseases," conditions which he said "were ripe with possibility." Metaphorically

speaking. Love as lupus. Unfortunately, many of these new diseases are related to the digestive and excretory systems.

"What kind of doctor's office is this?" I asked and he said: "The kind you can afford." The male nurse in the hallway snickered. "How old are you?" the doctor asked and shouted my reply down the hall. "She's my patient," he told a female nurse who looked wary. "I can ask my patient how old she is."

Well, he was not a doctor at all but one of the Lost Boys (Case 13-160), the loosely connected affiliate of young men on an international crime spree to wrestle away from me every woman they can (in marriage, if possible). They've gotten more sophisti-cated. Some have even started to dress better, and affect cultural attitudes which are clearly beyond their capabilities. ~AK

K:

I saw her. **xxxx**.

She was already surrounded when she walked in. I tried to help. Hello, I said. You should be dead, she said. Later she grabbed my ass and said she only pines for those at the news of their death. I begged her to come home with me (sorry) but she refused. She left with the bartender and two valets. I did not tell her you had survived.

Please advise.

—160

FOLLOW UP
International law forbids the import of any product that may:
1. console the inconsolable
2. change your life and your ways
3. contain a licorice (or other artificial or natural flavouring) from a country, person or affiliation believed to be Communist.

We can argue the last stipulation, but the first two, however obsolete, are still being enforced in several states. I think we have a seventy percent chance of bringing this to court and, if we can convince the judge that Love Block is not intended for mass-production but part of an ongoing experiment, we have a twenty percent chance of reprieve.

Of course, there are other venues. For sixty dollars a day, a clinic in the Ukraine will administer Love Block, along with a regimen of physical therapy and "aversive training" (beds modelled after Buchenwald). The clinic's matron saint, as she is referred to in the media, promises an unbelievable ninety percent rate of success, if love is caught in the first stages. After six months of untreated exposure, however, the numbers are more modest. At which point, she suggests only "temporal therapy." In six years, she says, regardless of treatment, all love is inevitably cured. ~AK

K:

I am confused. My dentist told me the problems with my teeth were genetic. She also told me, with the drill in my mouth, that the last time she knew love, he wore brass knuckles. I told her I would break his wrists.

It is pointless, she said, all crowns eventually crack.

Are you making strange dental analogies, I asked hopefully.

Open wider, she said, poking my wiggling gums.

You don't look very matronly, I slurred.

Strawberry or licorice?

What?

Fluoride. Don't you ever floss? She was visibly upset.

It's been three years since I've seen him, now he's dating a veterinar-
ian. Don't you have any Novocain?

It is in the drinking water. In another three years, you'll both
need a new set of teeth.

What? I spit.

You are most unlucky, she said in her thick Ukrainian accent.

Who? I drooled into her lap.

—160

🪝

160:
The sexual nature of dentistry: something the British
never learned. I admit I was aroused. The play of her
fingers in my mouth. Had it really been three years
since my last cleaning? A lie, but I nodded. And no one
has ever cleaned under your gums. Bite down. She
found three teeth I never knew I had, and left them
there. She said she had a boyfriend.

Has he shown you his rotten teeth? Once you see the
rotten teeth, it's impossible to feel anything but love
and disgust for someone, which are the same. ~K

K:

He would not show me his teeth, because at heart, Pigeon feared his toenails. They were black and green and yellow. I saw them the morning he forgot their cover and he cowered under my sheets. They are nothing, I said. Stop looking at them, he said. Truly, I felt nothing. But I killed him three times after that, in the way we should never kill. In that way the British used to do so that nothing, not even a tongue, survives.

—160

160:
The best lovers always have rotten toenails. I doubt anyone has seen **xxxx**'s toes. If it ever came close, she would switch feet.

There's an agent in Seattle, Special Operative Slinks, now researching an alternative to Love Block. Called "Wonder Love," this solution (currently available only as ingestible cream) contains quotes from Rilke on the label. The main ingredient is either olive oil or soy sauce. ~AK

I mailed **xxxx** a map and a compass and a plane ticket and a candy and a statement (notarized) of my eternal obsession. Was the candy excessive?

Operative O has suggested I close this file and continue to,.uh, work on the French maid. After all, we have a past (six days) and a future (Six days? I said and laughed. O didn't). Jeannette has a child: Cosimo, Cosmo for short. He has buggy eyes, just like mine and just like his mother's. He is five years older than me, which makes things...awkward.

When she is sixty, I will be thirty-five. When she is sixty-five...will she be sixty-five? You hear of it happening, but I haven't been around long enough to be sure it isn't a scam. I'll be lucky to make it to thirty.
~Agent K.

K:

The woman I am currently living with flew out of her room at four in the morning last night. The only way I can describe her flight is with that strange word, "frantic." You've got to be kidding me, she said into a phone, her black hair growing longer on the way to the door. Not

wanting to get involved, I went to my room with my burrito until I
was forced to answer a knock. One of those tall lanky boys came in
with a bloody rag around his head.

Were you a part of the revolution, I asked.

I was hit by a car, he said. Will you get my bike?

He fell on the couch next to my room. The woman turned her face to
me. We did not know each other yet like this. But such a look I had
given my father once.

I held up three fingers and he guessed correctly. I went to bed. (I am
the greatest protectress of those who link their destiny, even if
unknowingly, with mine. I would let him die, she is that precious.)

—160

🍃

160:
I didn't hit that bicyclist, and if I did, he probably
deserved it. Are you here? I realize you can't answer
that, but I feel like you're here.

I always hope that someone will crawl in the back
of my pickup while I'm parked. Someone will be

back there, someday. And then I remember that I
know no one in this city, not even myself.
Cigarette.
~K

★

K:

I quit smoking. I thought that would break the spell somehow. Like
smoke can be broken. He inhaled. I exhaled. He inhaled. I passed out.

★

My policy on age never changes: die young. No, die happy. Die with a
lot of possessions. Be buried with your lover's ear. I can never
remember. Probably because I never planned out a wedding as a
little girl.

I met Cosmo. He had lips like his mother. Operative O slapped me on the
wrist. Said I should only date older men if I wanted to go grey. I'm
already grey, I said. So you are, said O, closing my file. Now, let's talk
about the inherent excessiveness of candy. Candy isn't inherent, I

pointed out. (I always feel the need to point out bad science.) The stickiness of genetics. O fumbled his cigarette. Your review is in six months, he said.

—160

Operative O:
I understand your concern, but I object to the use of the words "melodramatic" and "florid" with regard to our submitted reports. This case is still very much in progress and Agent 160 and I are simply exploring every avenue at our disposal to ensure proper handling.

If the result is, at times, "less than lucid," I argue that this is the nature of the case and that a more "straightforward" accounting procedure would in fact not only deceive, but prove more confusing, ultimately.

Are we attempting to find what we are looking for or have we "wandered onto some other mess along the way?" I have not sufficiently answered this question for my own personal purposes, let alone from the standpoint of this case, which, might I remind you, is not my job.

We intend to proceed without delay and ask that you wait until Monday to post conclusions and, if necessary, make reprimands.

Yours sincerely,
Agent K.

160:
I carbon copied you in my message to O. He doesn't have a toe to stand on, so to speak. In one of these boxes I've still got the film from Reno and, if I ever find it and get around to developing it, well...

I'm surprised we've never met, 160. Why is it called a carbon copy? Isn't carbon a sign of organic life? ~K

K:

Thank you for the message. I will say, however, we are playing with some kind of fire. (Proverbial, metaphorical, illegal.) Operative O is an uncanny visionary, some say with the ability to see the future. (See self-filed resumé.) If O is worried about our reports, perhaps it is with good reason. Because of this good reason we should completely distrust/disregard his criticism. Every visionary is biased to their future. We're just not sure if we have one.

Are you sure we haven't met? Perhaps you should find that film, Agent K.

—160

160:
Now I'm embarrassed. How could I have forgotten you, along with the entire state of South Dakota? I agree about O. Against his orders, I've been searching the files for cases that might relate to ours. Under: love, failed, I found over 7,000 cases listed. Cross-referenced for love, unrequited, brought our numbers up to 10,000. This is just among other agents.

The reference librarian at Headquarters West, Miss Plum, is this psychotically nice, little mousy woman who looks like she's been sitting at the same desk, in the same clothes, since 1976.

I pointed out that ours is probably the only library on the Coast that doesn't have a computer, heck, most are practically automated these days (I did say heck. Plum's influence), and she said, "Computer?" and repeated the word several times before writing it out on a notecard in teacher's cursive, followed by: *find out*.

You're not allowed to bring even a pen into the "holding room," where they keep all the old love and hate letters (divided into said categories, with an even larger "inde-terminate" section dividing them). Plum explained that this is because the desire to edit said documents, should you come upon any with yourself as the subject or even the object, was "a natural temptation." That's why it's against the rules to purposefully and meaning-fully search for anyone you know. "These letters are meant for novelty use only."

You know what that means. I went straight for the files of everyone I know, as did everyone else. The sound of sobbing, amplified by vaulted ceilings, would have been deafening, were I not already deafened by the click of a hundred electric typewriters—the purpose of which, ostensibly, was to allow non-pencil note-taking—but upon which typists were writing additional notes, rejoin-ders and accusations, which they blatantly re-filed.

I didn't want to be too obvious about pulling the files I really wanted to see—girlfriends of people I'd dated or wanted to—so I'd take the whole sub-section.

"Finding everything you need?" Plum would ask, as a sort of passive-aggressive deterrent. Obviously, this

must happen all the time. I don't know why else the
grocery carts were there.

Plum presided over the room from an elevated marble
desk, which held a book stand, which held a leather-
bound copy of *Jane Eyre* with gold lettering. She
coughed twice each time she turned a page.

The Jeannette lust file has its own section of a library in
Pomona, but I was surprised and relieved to find only
two love files on her: myself and another woman. Both
contained a lot of overwrought poetry with too many
mentions of skin. Which sort of made me fall for her all
over again.

Anyway, I didn't even get to our files. I have some
surveillance to do tomorrow morning (Farley case) and
I'll try to stop by again in the afternoon. ~K

Agent K:
Headquarters East, run by Miss Rose, was unnerving in the same
manner. Though she serves small chocolates on little plates, we all
know that they are meant to be a torturous aphrodisiac in her own
twisted version of love offered then guilted. In the large holding room,
there was a row of daggers, which I took to be very sexist, but in
actuality they were just fancy letter openers. Above the door was a

moving sign that said in tiny, red lights: Letters never sent on presumption of death, shame or cowardice. Or good measure.

Does anyone still believe in the psychological model of purging? It suddenly seemed suspicious. I ate six chocolates while looking up all the envelopes addressed to me. (Strange to see my real name.) There were only five. As I unwittingly got chocolate fingerprints on them, I had to steal them, which was very easy as Miss Rose apparently spends a lot of time in the bathroom.

The first two envelopes were bills. My postman had died, I supposed, with his bag still around his shoulder. I tossed them in the shredder. The next letter was from my mother, with a twenty dollar bill, creased calmly, in the centre. She had died too, with something in her hand. There are two more, which remain unopened as I water my garden.

—160

160:
I'm very sorry to hear about your mother. Are you sure your mother didn't set the letter aside and then, for complicated and mysterious reasons, fail to send it? I know when I fail to send letters it's usually for complicated and mysterious reasons, even to me. A lack of communication could indicate

any number of things: indifference, sadness, bad weather, low blood sugar.

I've always had sort of a crush on Miss Rose. She's got that push/pull thing down, so you're always left wanting whatever she's not willing to offer. She said I reminded her of a younger version of herself, which I took to mean: I would sleep with you but you terrify me.

In my experience, everyone looks for someone just like themselves, but what they really want is someone just like some portion of themselves, more manageable, a clumsy copy. When the copy is too close, you get in stubborn fights, which are really stubborn fights with yourself, and you resent them in ways you never would yourself. Things get complicated and rambling, much like this letter.

So you have a real name? Mine is legally Agent. Which means my parents were both Agent. Which means at least I have or had parents. Sometimes I wonder about that.

Do you want the two letters destroyed? Please advise. ~K

p.s. Were there any letters for me?

🪶

K:

While I was stationed in Reno, an elderly man with frizzy hair on both sides of his head paid me fifty bucks to sit in a hot tub with his young son. Since I only managed to win twenty bucks at roulette, I sighed and put on his wife's oversized bathing suit, complete with full skirt. His son was only eighteen, emaciated and quite drunk. (I have only seen one person ever look the way he did, he was propped up against a tree and died a short time later.)

It is so distilled, this kind of party.

The boy had been sleeping in the vineyards and his dust settled on the bottom of the hot tub between my toes. I was quite young.

Did you meet my parents? he asked.

Yes, I said.

Do you know what the highest compliment is for someone you love?

No.

To miss them, even when you are together.

When he looked too grey and dry, I put him to bed and re-entered the neon chambers.

★

Agent K:

I will tell you who first introduced me to the martyrdom of love. For most, I believe, it is similar. When you first realize you would pull out your own veins to feed your sister.

Can I blame her, then?
Or would that be my parents?

They are smart creatures to link themselves to us through an unsuspecting child.

—Agent 160

★

MOTION TO EXTEND
a preliminary report submitted by agent(s) K. and
160

Through extensive fieldwork, surveillance and the
scavenging of records both private and public,
Agent 160 and myself have attempted, over the
past (less than twenty-four hours), to explain the
entire history, including our own places within
(subject in question)(love).

We are quite pleased with the work done so far, and
even more pleased with ourselves and each other,
as we have never taken on a project of this scope
and import. However, (subject in question) remains
so elusive that we have, as of yet, found neither the
answers, if available, nor a confident list of questions.
We respectfully request an extension. More tests are
necessary.
Signed,
(real name) aka Agent 160
Agent K.

Agent K:

Miss Rose said there had been a stack for you, but they were stolen. I
figured it had been you. I'll see what I can do. Perhaps someone knows
something. I am sure they will turn up.

My fifth letter self-destructed. (Obviously someone too smart to be of any interest.) The other letter blew onto the train tracks. A dog got it wet when he retrieved it, so I took him home. Now they are both drying.

Miss Rose said she hasn't seen you lately. I said you may be in town soon. Did I blow your cover? I think I blew it. What is it about these librarians? You should wear a disguise. My real name went along with my real life. So at least they have company.

The last time I loved someone exactly like myself, we became brothers.

Do not worry about my mother. She would be happy I got the twenty bucks.

Sincerely,

Agent 160

160
Rose doesn't exist. I invented her; the first mistake.

Then we both invented her. Does this mean we have the power to
change the world? Someone is laughing outside my window.

🔻

K:

One night I was playing pool with Ralph, the manager of a motel I was
living in for a short while. (Such places one only gets to live
in, never "staying at.") Into the second game (I won the first,
of course) Ralph let it slip that the owners of the motel wanted him to
kick out the woman operating a bordello that so happened to be down
the hall from my room.

The same woman had recently given me an Easter basket full of tiny
tinfoil chocolates.

She had borrowed a room key from Ralph and set it on my bed. It had
been my birthday present.

I'm carrying a firearm, I told him.

He sighed. You are much too young for this.

You are much too old and wearing too much flannel for this. Plus,
nothing is illegal in Nevada, I reminded him.

Nothing is illegal for tourists in Nevada, he reminded me.

Everyone was a tourist here, at one time, I said to the cue ball.

It is hard to find a wife here, he said after a long pause, to the eight ball.

Later I planned out my next mission (gambling route) (escape) while he tried to pick up the waitress.

—160

160:
Everyone tries to pick up the waitress. I'm just not that interested in food. Enclosed please find: sleeping pills, a half-empty bottle of old wine and something you already own, in a new material (glass). The clerk promised it's shatter-proof, but obviously I wasn't going to test it. She had that butch attitude that made it impossible to glean anything but condescension and annoyance. Total bottom.
Oh, and the bottled scent of my cat yawning. Let me know if it works. Any of it. ~K

Agent K:

The waitress has to be the shittiest role ever given. I won't stare at a waiter's dick unless I trip over it. And even then it is just to hold something till I get off, er, up.

I can't wait to pleasure myself with my new glass-blowing art, while I smell a cat bored with my effort. You should write off that expense to Operative O as *glass, dolphin*.

—160

160:
If I'm not mistaken, the budget only allows one "glass, dolphin" a month, and it wasn't a completely altruistic errand. Cheers? ~K

K:

In that case, I will use it both selfishly and altruistically.

Cheers.

160

p.s.

The woman who stole your letters is a woman. She is of a of certain height and weight with a certain hair colour. Do you know her? Do you want me to retrieve the letters? If they were all written by her, perhaps you already know what they say. But that is only me, pretending I know your business outside of knowing what I know as being an agent, clearly marked by the word before my secret number. I will butt out now as your fellow agent-comrade-colleague-spearhead-thingy.

160:
I appreciate your offer. I have no official business with a woman of a certain height and weight with a certain hair colour. I'm sure she'd say the same. Of course, independently, every agent is free to conduct business with who or whomever they desire. Glass, dolphin.

Of course, I'm in love with her. Glass, dolphin.

Does love deliver letters? (No glass, too predictable.) Does love have anything to do with letters?

Please burn the letters, the love, if combustible—

assuming either was ever sent or rescinded in the first place. ~K.

p.s. No boy is too smart for you. Please forward the updated list of wrists to break.

Someone must have been telling lies about Agent K., for one morning, without having done anything truly wrong, she was arrested.

The charges against her: moral turpitude, wallowing, borrowing the occasional line from Kafka, all seemed reasonable, though she had received them in a questionable email (in between "you too can be smart" and "watch woman taste her own...").

There was an immediate knock on the door, and K remembered she had recently stolen a traveller's outfit, whatever that was. She put it on.

160: Is this Operative O's idea of a joke?
It is possible we will:
a. never finish this report
b. never want to finish this report
c. finish it, and never find anything else that comes close
Please advise ~AK

p.s. O wants to know how many pages we have and who we want to play ourselves in the movie version of our lives. I suggested it was still rather early in the report, not to mention presumptuous, to begin thinking of such things and he said: "That's exactly the kind of attitude that will never make you rich and famous."

It was an uncomfortable situation. Literally. The traveller's underwear was riding up my ass (whoever decided that travelling is best accomplished in a thong?) and off in the distance, for whatever reason, ten to twenty alarm clocks were going off simultaneously. "Experimental elevator music," O pointed out. As with most men, I can never tell when he's trying to be intentionally funny.

Anyway, so I said Scarlett Johansson for you, Cary Grant for me. Then he said, living, they must be living, so I said, fine, Scarlett for you, Scarlett for me. And then he said, You know Agent K., sometimes I wonder if you two are retarded. I have a whole file of IQ tests on you, and all of them suggest the opposite, but sometimes I wonder if the top of the scale circles back to the bottom...Shut up, shut up, shut up, shut up. (That isn't what he said. That's what I was thinking about the alarm clock music.)

The next thing I heard, several minutes later was:

It's always in one ear and right out the other with you, K...a vigilante streak...and your friend...a martyr complex.

Some of this may have been the two televisions in the room, both playing that terrible doctor show, the one that doesn't star Christine Lahti. Stat.

Dear Operative O:

I have a few aces I am keeping in the hole of my new martyrdom skirt!

This morning I saw the emperor wearing the same one and the embarrassment drove me home.

These were in my jeans:

1) We have enough pages to make a small paper boat to sail down the Thames.

2) The Thames has swallowed more disgruntled lovers than the Golden Gate.

3) I picture you with long flowing locks, like Samson or Delilah.

4) You are not thinking of us.

—Agent 160

160:
He will eat his words, along with that box of doughnuts I brought as a distraction in the event that the "important meeting" was another attempt to make a pathetic pass at me. (What part of: girls, girls, girls does O fail to understand?)

Your Golden Gate comment reminds me of something I eavesdropped recently; that the survivors of amazing falls, from planes or bridges, have this in common: a childhood (or later) removal of the appendix. Perhaps this is also what marks the difference between those who survive love, admittedly broken, and the rest of us, at the bottom of a river, or wherever we are.

I'm making an appointment to have my appendix removed, along with my spleen, because I've never enjoyed the word "spleen" and no one has ever made a convincing argument for its continued

occupation. I did a report once in school, "your
spleen, your friend," and I can remember vaguely
that the spleen looks like a lima bean, or maybe I just
said that because lima beans were easy to find and
hand out as we were required to utilize a visual aid.

I'd also like to remove my brain, that grumpy prune.
But my doctor insists that without a brain, I would
not be alive, and if I was not alive, I would not pay my
bill. And thus, for "ethical reasons," he always declines.

To Whom It May Concern:

Without Agent K. I will be unable to continue our project. We have
been partially honest, fed our pets, and waited for a sunny day. Our
report, if we survive to the end, will be what we could not have
thought of. I am sure you understand. Whatever Agent K. has done,
rest assured she will not be able to admit it. I mean undo it. Operative
O holds us quite strictly to time and space. And we listen. But, there
is not a dry bone in her body.

Thank you.

Agent 160

Forgive me, I was raised in a barn. 160: please meet my attractive new assistant, Associate Agent Kelli. Kelli paid my bail, which begins an even longer story. She may have been one of the many reasons I was arrested, finally.

Before your mind wanders unsavoury paths related to minors, I must first confess: my "crimes" are all vehicular. Beyond that, of course, I can't comment because of the pending trial. But it's common knowledge that I drive, and do many things, very, very quickly. Some who know me in limited ways assume I'm generally incapable of variations in speed and rhythm. Not so! Not so! Cover your ears, Kelli. (She's not even here. She's wandered back into the bedroom.)

Where was I? My assistant. So they're leading me into the PD, and I'm anticipating invasive, humiliating searches. You know, procedures to which, under ordinary circumstances, I would look forward.

O is yammering into his cell phone, ordering either a plane ticket or a pizza. I slip him a twenty and he suddenly remembers: "You can't arrest her! Agent K. is scheduled to host a citizen ride-along today. Part of the new Contemporary Community Standards project."

I can't host a citizen ride-along, I protest, during our smoke break. I am a secret (key word: secret) agent.

But then I see the young lady, sitting shotgun in my pickup (which has now been outfitted with a new high-tech device to remind me when I am going too fast, something known among civilian circles as a speedometer).

She's Wow. Blonde, hygienic, perfect teeth, whip smart. She exudes no obvious signs of: sadism, mental illness, indecisiveness, mixed signals, defensiveness, general confusion about life in all its aspects. So, in other words, not someone I would ever become involved with.

Luckily, she already has a much younger friend, a little stoner, Scooter. By stoner I am also alluding to Scooter's gender—inconclusive—and career—same. They've been at it all afternoon in my office. There was a brief break when the doorbell rang—Scooter's drug dealer. Then after they kept knocking each other over in the shower, then left for a short while, muttering something about falafel.
Any progress on your end? I promise I will get something done as soon as I rid myself of this electronic monitoring device. ~AK

Agent K:

Miss Rose stormed into my apartment this morning while I was painting it pinkish-purple. She accused me of stealing. These weren't meant to be seen, she said. But you have a gallery, I said. Exactly, she countered. I gave the letters to her, obviously opened by a canine. Who are they from, she finally asked. Stephen Hawking for one.

I reproduced for you the part that is of interest to our project.

Because the partial theories that we already have are sufficient to make accurate predictions in all the most extreme situations...the discovery of a complete unified theory...may not even affect our (bite marks, water stain).

I like to think he was going to say love, but we had never even met. Apparently, I need glasses.

Rose gave her final analysis: You are spreading lies.

—Agent 160

Dear O:

I would like to submit that this project is making me a better person.
It cleans my dishes, washes my leg hair, earns the woman whom I am
currently living with's undying respect.

Did you know that when Medusa's hair bled on the floor, out sprang
Pegasus?

It is true that I have been spreading lies. But then again, only lies.
Then again, only letters. Then again.

—160

Agent 160:
My apartment is greenish, greyish, yuckish. Why is it
always "spread" lies and never "redistribute" or "relo-
cate"? Are lies peanut butter?

I showed your picture (craps table, your shirt still

on) to my squirrels, and Scooter says you are "one hot mama." You are also old enough to be Scooter's mama, though Scooter didn't point this out. S/he is savvy enough to know love math. Though s/he will never catch you in age, s/he may get "close enough."

This seemed like bad math when Jeannette explained it to me, but it's true. When I was born, she was twenty-five times as old as me. Now, she's only twice as old as me. I wish that meant something. Do you have any children of your own, agent? This can influence the equation. If I was a man, I would have a child in every state, named after the capital.

Agent Montgomery, Agent Juneau, Agent Phoenix, Agent Little Rock, Agent Sacramento, Agent Denver, Agent Hartford, Agent Dover, Agent Tallahassee, Agent Atlanta, Agent Honolulu, Agent Boise, Agent Springfield, Agent Indianapolis, Agent Des Moines, Agent Topeka, Agent Frankfort, Agent Baton Rouge, Agent Augusta, Agent Annapolis, Agent Boston, Agent Lansing, Agent St. Paul, Agent Jackson, Agent Jefferson City, Agent Helena, Agent Lincoln, Agent Carson City, Agent Concord, Agent Trenton, Agent Santa Fe, Agent Albany, Agent Raleigh, Agent Bismarck, Agent Columbus, Agent Oklahoma City,

Agent Salem, Agent Harrisburg, Agent Providence, Agent Columbia, Agent Pierre, Agent Nashville, Agent Austin, Agent Salt Lake City, Agent Montpelier, Agent Richmond, Agent Olympia, Agent Charleston, Agent Madison, Agent Cheyenne.

Everyone will have a different response to my potential children's names. For instance, (Agent) Honolulu could be where an old love lives. If I met a young lady named Agent Honolulu (this assuming it was not one of my many children, but another Agent Honolulu, what a coincidence!), I might be more friendly towards her. Not friendly in a creepy way.

Agent Bismarck: where I was born. According to the files.

I'm still trying to calculate in which of these states I have yet to have sex. When I was travelling more, I kept a little map for this purpose, but it got depressing. It can be depressing, when one's standards automatically eliminate 99.999% of the human race. A little chemical assistance and the number drops to about 97%, but you always regret it, whether immediately, or years later. ~K

Agent K:

How strange you should guess my heritage. My real name is the
capital of Alabama. Don't tell Operative O, he would fly there immediately and send me little spoons and shot glasses. Don't worry, he
doesn't turn out to be my father.

Children speak nonsense. In other words, they know too much. That
is why it took me so long to make up a dog. I knew he would know.
And then he did and he fell asleep on my feet. What did you do drug
him, my friend Stacks asked. But I hadn't.

If a child fell asleep on my feet I would turn to statue, forcing her to
wake up, crack me open and look inside. (Very much like that old
story of Rachel and the idol.) And what would she find? What would
she find? A small talking woman? Can I choose the group option?
Scooter and Kelli and the two kitties? Jeannette used to say we
could have two little girls who wore cowboy hats and raised each
other.

The woman whom I am currently living with said she was going to go down (where?) to freeze her eggs. That after thirty-two, fertility is halved. Maybe medical school isn't good for anyone. I would pick out the freezer that never got sad. Or cleaned.

I showed my dog the picture of you off your website that the police had to take down for "too much fun in a pickup." He thought it was really interesting.

 I'm sending you a photograph of a site where someone is building something that loosely translates into "love, blockened."

I need directions.

—Agent 160

🥾

You're named after a capital? Are we thinking with the same brain, 160? If so, I hope it's yours.

You had imaginary children with Jeannette too? Did the neighbours complain about the noise?

I'm confused about this site. Love Block is a nuclear
reactor? Advise. ~K

p.s. You can never have too much fun in a pickup.

K:

The woman whom I am currently living with is having sex down the
hall with injured bike head. The thing is, I hear only him. I'd rather
hear only her. I am getting arrested at this very moment. Arrested by
something called horniness.

Also, our horoscopes the agency sends out says I'm dead and there-
fore not written in the Book of Eternal Life (surprise) and that you
have been arrested for supposedly teaching a man to fish who later
died of starvation. I'm assuming you are a Capricorn?

—160

160:

xxxx might say: join them. I say: wait until you have all the information. Though I can't count how many women I've lost by this method. Waiting is always a solitary activity, regardless of what anyone tells you. ~K

Agent K:

Well, it's definitely not Nevada (sorry, Carson City). I don't think that it is a nuclear reactor. Though Stephen Hawking wrote, in a happy tone, partial theories of the universe were able to create nuclear energy. I am not sure how that relates to us. I have also forgotten if we are supposed to find Love Block, apply it, or destroy it. I think it is my hardened Agent edge coming out. Or Miss Rose told me that he is starting a new life in California and would find the perfect wife and have the perfect life and have so many babies they would have to give some away.

(To be offensive is to be empathetic.)

—Agent 160

160:
Pigeon will never survive without you. His marriage will be a tedious enactment of this failure.

Like so much bad architecture, the Love Block building looks a lot like a penis. I don't know where I got nuclear reactor from. I thought Love Block would make us high. I mean, "chemically shield one from the fallout caused by love," or however I wrote it in the proposal. I lost all of that paperwork. ~K

PROGRESS REPORT
Operative O:
Due to sexual frustration, time delays, house arrest, and the notorious activities and interference of other people, Agent 160 and myself hereby request a second extension on this, our non-tortured, but possibly torturous study of (subject confidential) (love).

In addition, we hereby request the disclosure of all bordellos situated within a reasonable distance of zip codes: 60622 (Chicago, Illinois) and 97219 (Portland, Oregon). Please omit any such business in which agent is resident. This is an internal investigative matter that should not further concern you.

Please also forward all reports, gossip, rumours and innuendos concerning the following substance and/or structure: Love Block.

Appreciate it.
~Madame K.

Agent K:

It turns out the site was actually the Eiffel Tower. You would think that France would have been more helpful in our search. I know when I was 16, it was very helpful.

As I can't read Ukrainian and my dentist mysteriously disappeared, I think researching bordellos is an excellent idea. I will buy alcohol at the dive down the street whose remaining neon lights spell c-h-i-l-d.

There is a new interest on the street. His name is Cup. Unfortunately, our mission may render him obsolete, I mean the whole idea/thing too boring. Chemically stable. Like wood. Unlike water. He offered to put in a pool. No one from Michigan knows how to swim, I told him.

I may hire him as a surveillance team instead. Or as a suspect.

Pigeon had a Great Dane who loved me like a sister.
His name was Luther.

It is a harsh world and I only know how to make spaghetti/mix
whiskey.

The bordello down my street is called Miss Hannigan's.
0 recommended it.

—160

Agent 160:
What is it with bordellos and Dickens references? I
don't know how I feel about how literate sex has

become lately. Sorry I missed your call. I was masturbating. I've missed several of your calls for this reason. I don't know what that says about the frequency of either event. I guess we're both fortunate that the agency is too cheap to invest in a proper video-phone system.

Before that, I spent several hours drinking and admiring my new anklet/tracking device. I'm not much for jewellery, but it's foxy-silver with a complicated pattern that either is a computer chip or imitates a computer chip. Astrea (cat) finally chewed it off. I thought it might make a nice collar, but the cat had other plans, as cats do. Now Kelli's wearing it and, judging by the noises coming out of the office, I have to agree with what the officer said about it being the least inhibiting of tracking options.

Which is all just to say that there is no reason why I'm still in the apartment and not out doing fieldwork. Well, there are many reasons. One: I had this feeling that **xxxx** might be in my town and, if she is in my town, that she might ring the doorbell.

Where to even begin with this illogical little fantasy of mine. First of all, I don't even have a doorbell. ~AK

Agent K:

A breakthrough. Sort of.

Miss Hannigan herself claims to use the generic brand of Love Block, which comes in a spray. However, when I pressed her about it, she would only say that it does not follow the old less-is-more trope. So more is less? Less what, I asked. Less headache, she said. Heartache? Turn the music up, she said to no one in particular. After we danced, she turned to me and—I swear this is true and not the whiskey talking—she evaporated, fishnets and all (I had the same ones in hot pink and I was not embarrassed at all). Like the alternate ending to the Helen of Troy myth. What's that guy's name, Achilles or something. And he finds her in Egypt and he talks to her and she evaporates before his eyes. He started the whole Trojan war based on a rumour. That she was in Egypt. Helen.

So anyway, Miss Hannigan evaporates. Perhaps generic is not as good. But by all means, keep taking your medication.

—Agent 160

160:
There are few, if any, women in this world I would
start a war over. I can't tell if that indicates optimism
or pessimism or gin.

I'm hoping for an earthquake, or any geological sign to
let me know, finally and for sure: give up. I can't take
personal responsibility for any actions originating
from a source as small and unsanctioned as myself. To
whom may I complain when I fuck up?

Why I moved west: volcanoes, earthquakes, any
number of disasters could end this, along with all
evidence my housekeeping has always been this poor.
Have you ever had sex during an earthquake? It's
not much different. The hangers knock against each
other, which is really only distracting for whoever's
staring into the closet.

Agent Bird, he's not on solid ground. I don't know if
that's comforting but it's true. ~AK

K:

Solid ground is a fly on the screen. To nature. The Midwest has wind, ground and a tornado.

However, the tornado never comes to the city.

Does it fear heights?

Does it have to be the tallest thing in a room?

I do protest the lack of movement. Here.

If there was a good mountain range, I feel I would not get so lonely.

Pigeon used to say whenever he feels lost he goes to the edge of a

large body of water and he knows where he is.

The lake here is mum, mum, mum.

This is what I know, I am away from.

—160

160:
Mountains are lonely too, but not as lonely as rivers.
Trees want us to feel bad we don't have more
friends. Concrete loves and is dependent on us.
Which gets tiring.

The city where I live has six bridges. That's not
another corny statement, just means it will take too
long to get to the bordello, and I'm too drunk. ~K

K:

Bridges are paraphernalia of a pretend journey. I suggest you only
cross one a day if you can help it. Has xxxx arrived?

The building of the Mackinaw Bridge (five miles long) did not cost one
life. It is a kind of ad. I used to think I could feel her in a room and
then one day she was there and I was waiting outside and she met
her husband in that place.

There is one love that I could not block. No, that's not true. Clarice
Lispector said anguish in the young is compassion for the world. I
feel this cigarette, my last prop.

—160

160:

What the cartoons don't teach you is that angels and devils are not distributed in pairs. Mistakes are made. Some get a cartoon devil on either shoulder, and some get two angels. And of this group, some people, I would argue, the best people, think they have double devils when in fact they have two angels, irritable or taking on a tough pose for effect (often at the wearer's suggestion).

This might sound like children's business, but a false angel/devil dynamic, even a perceived false angel/devil dynamic, can lead to disaster in imaginary love, which is the most genuine strain.

And if that isn't convoluted enough, cartoons are fickle and change with the times. It's almost impossible to correctly perceive your own cartoon guardians, which is why problems in this area are often first discovered by a lover.

Let's leave religion out of it. Angels and devils are easier to draw and more standardized than other representations of our good and bad motivations. Once you open it up to interpretation, some people will want sports mascots. Or, more appallingly, people they know, who—due to the miniaturization/simplification—are easy to manipulate.

Where am I going with this, agent? She's a double-angel. Hers are an advanced version, as evidenced

by their wicked smiles. **xxxx** would deny this.
People this perceptive always overlook the obvious.
But I know, and this is proof, because any double
devil would be here by now. ~AK

K:

I have known two double-angels.

Should I tell them,

I know where they are, at all times?

—160

160:
There's a possibility that Love Block does not exist.
No, it is all too real. Keep walking. If your love
(person, thing) is imaginary, shouldn't the cure be
equally imaginary? No one dies in their dreams. You
love an imaginary person and confuse them for
someone walking. You see an actor on the street
and call them by their tv name. This has all been
documented already by numerous people who
never saw a tv.

Which is to say, maybe we have found Love Block,

and Love Block is this report, but even so, it will only
work if our love is imaginary. And who can know if
their love is imaginary?

I'm not throwing these questions at you to make
my brain seem big, or more mottled, I'm just
suggesting phase two of the investigation: is love
real? And specifically, is ours?

I hope I'm wrong on this one. I'd much prefer a
spray or ointment, something only found on a tropi-
cal island with coconuts for bras. I hate when
missions conclude conclusively. It makes me think
we might be doing our job or something.

Let me know what you think. ~AK

Agent K:

I wish I fell more in my dreams.

Instead there is a lot of hand holding and a general milling about and

a waiting for things to drop. Besides me, I mean. Besides me.

—160

p.s. Homeopathy believes that like cures like. One imaginary love to fix another. When your symptoms from the new imaginary love match the old ones closely enough, both will disappear. That is the price of such a remedy.

Agent 160:
I hope I haven't offended you with my portentous (pretentious) little letters. I'm hung over, obviously. I've been thinking of how we could market Love Block, if it turns out to be nothing. Love Block: your problems are imaginary and so are our solutions. Beats Rilke? ~AK

Agent K:

I began to get suspicious, as I watched a tornado pass through town last night, that perhaps we were not the only agents on this mission. And if so, perhaps they have succeeded years ago and the exact abstract proportions of Love Block have been lost in numerous paper trails through out the history of pulp.

If this is true, all recent contact with A-Z have been repetitions of some other happiness/loss, already gone.

—160

Will you come to my trial, Agent 160? As a voyeur, if you want, but mainly I'm inviting you because I think you're the only one who can be of any help The judge likes you. Sometimes I think the judge likes you because she gets awkward when she talks about you, and does that tic where she compulsively repeats the same statement a dozen times, as if trying to convince herself, the last holdout. Also, she closes her eyes, and fidgets more than usual.

I imagine my trial will either continue as it has been, in ways that are neither apparent nor satisfying, but still always leaving just enough hope that one is able to fill in what's missing with whiskey.

Or, that because of this report a rapid conclusion will be necessitated, thus provided. Our report flung across the room. A paper cut from which I will never recover. This ending too could never be satisfying because it is unnatural, my own forced conclusion, which I have already attempted once, in a conversation that contained few words.

Is it torture to provoke someone to speak? Certainly by our standards, by the Geneva Conventions. But I can't find anything in the manual that says it is prohibited in Fictional France. Request for a change of venue. ~Agent K.

AK:

Change of venue granted. Fictional France is always up for a good trial, but everyone must wear a costume representing the memory of their imaginary love.

The only useful advice I have ever given: It has been my experience in the courtroom that if one is guilty, it is best to request a jury. Guilt cut in twelve ways equals innocence.

However, innocence cut one way equals jail time.

However, jail time in Fictional France has the advantage of the limit-experience.

The current judge sounds like a toss up, considering she closes her eyes when you are within the contact distance of two feet. For the record, I have never even seen her blink.

I will be there with braids in my hair.

My dog will be there dressed like a cat. Or a lion, he says.

Also: we need witnesses. And counter-witnesses.

And the last line should be: we flew off into the sunset in a silver toy.

—160

160:
I was just wondering what I should wear to the trial. Jeans? Or jeans? Jeans, I think.

Last night when I was drunk, I was staring into the mirror and I didn't recognize myself, and neither did my devil/angels. Am I a reliable witness on my own behalf?

There's no room for a sunset in this report. ~AK

AK:

Why do I find it easier to continue our quest with a sucker in my mouth?

Perhaps Love Block is like Botox, you look puffy for a while and then the lines redraw themselves.

Do our own appearances deceive us?

—160

160:
Love Block is aesthetic and necessary, and should be covered by health insurance around the time they start paying for birth control. Though it's also addictive, and unproven, over the long term.   ~AK

AK:

They now have birth control as a patch. Perhaps we are thinking of quitting?

The newest birth control is in ring form. On the website you can test its flexibility by pinching it.

It is an illusion, a ring is always a ring.

—160

160:
Bridges are flexible so that they don't crack under
pressure. Skyscrapers, same. Love, on the other
hand, was engineered under an old and obsolete
safety model. If your love was made before 1975, the
current regulations may not apply.

I am out of drugs and toilet paper. Which is one
item short of leaving the house. In addition, your
computer just sent notice that it's dumping you.
Was it something I said, I asked, and it said: even I
can think of a better line that that, and I have only
forty or so lines to choose from.

Listen, I told it, shape up or ship out. Send me back
my agent friend, or I will turn into your mother.

You're not my mother, your computer said. My mother
has nine pounds of lead in her head and is sitting in
some trash heap, which is also a village, in Indonesia.

Well, I felt like an ass. At the same time, it's an old trick, using unrelated tragedy to elicit confused sympathy for whatever terrible thing you're currently doing. A lot of modifiers there. But you get the idea.

So, I don't know if you'll get this message or not, 160. I don't know if I'm even typing this. Coming down from drugs, it's just a lot of sweating and listening to yourself talk. ~AK

Operative O:
I appreciate the concern, but I can assure you that Agent 160 is not "intentionally incommunicado." As we speak, a team of elite specialists is taking apart her entire life, er, computer, trying to salvage whatever might be left.

Have I ever told you about the Moment of Despair, Operative? Well, it's something that I either discovered or that someone told me about and that I now remember and repeat verbatim as my own theory. Probably the latter.

It goes like this: three quarters of the way through any movie, there is a false ending, where it seems like "all hope is lost," "everything is pointless," you've run out of toilet paper and even run through all the usable "seconds" in the garbage can.

The Moment of Despair is often accompanied by swelling music. You spend the next twenty minutes in your seat, wriggling and yawning, wanting to pee, or wanting popcorn, or wanting all sorts of things you want when things should be over, sex.

It's not the end. You want it to be the end. Frankly, you'd rather be in bed. Frankly, not even with whoever you've dragged to this freezing, sticky cavern. Which means, also, you've just wasted twenty bucks.

I forget what my point was with this. Oh yeah, this isn't the end. So fuck off.
~K

Dear Operative O:

I find your notice of firing me for a younger, curvier, more technologically savvy version of myself too obvious to be plausible.

Plus, you work for us.

As it so happens, the moment of despair can end at any other moment.

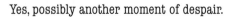

In effect, something else happens.

Yes, possibly another moment of despair.

This still—life.

You learn this lesson when you are plastered to your bed or your wall or your coffee mug for years at a time.

You learn this lesson when nothing is blocking you from anything or anyone else.

Do I sound polemic?

It is really a plea.

—Agent 160

♠

K:

Operative O says I'm to be your defense lawyer!

For your prosecutor you can choose between three people and they can even be dead.

Vive la Fictional France.

—160

160:
Welcome back, Agent! Replacement? I'm going to pretend I didn't hear that. Although a woman knocked on my door a few hours ago and demanded a complete case history, along with post-coital photo collection. Post-coital photo collection? I said. You're either meticulous or...

"I like to know who I'm working with," she said and propped her legs up on my knee. She was wearing a t-shirt that said "yummy." As it turned out, she wasn't an agent at all but a "potential client," and not even of mine, but of yours. Her plane touches down at eight; don't be late.

Trial update: I found several witnesses who will admit to not seeing anything, though they were aware of what wasn't going on. Does this make them unreliable as witnesses?

Also, your, uh, deliveries are being routed to me. I've received several packages from Pigeon, or someone claiming to be him. I ate the cheese platter. Didn't know when you'd be back. ~Agent K.

Agent K:

That sounds like her.

Did you see any devils?

She has a t-shirt that says Justice on it.

I like to find my own jury.

—160

K:

My surveillance team is getting antsy for some movement.

Where should you go today? I asked.

We put an ad in the paper saying we lost "Love Block" and would like

to be reunited.

I read about the technique in a Sherlock Holmes book but I'm not too

hopeful it will work. If someone had it, why would they give it up?

Unless they don't know what it is.

Which puts them right in the centre of our investigation.

—Agent 160

160:

I answered your ad. I thought it might be one of O's tricks to see if I'm actually working or just checking my email all day. Which, obviously, since I answered the ad, means... Anyway, disregard the message from the goat herder.

I don't think newspaper ads are going to get us any closer to Love Block. Likewise, we probably won't find it in bars. Whoever has this stuff is either in a hot tub at the bunny ranch right now, or is the kind of person who spends his Labour Day in a university library, nose wrinkled in concentration as he writes crabbed notes all over page 377 of his dissertation on Goncharov's *Oblomov*.

The list of people immune from love. We could spend the next five years compiling this and still not find anyone decent to hook up with. Perhaps we should narrow it down to women. Hot, available women. Or whatever sorting system you think works best. I can't wait until the pharmacy opens back up tomorrow. ~AK

Agent K:

I hope you're feeling all right because I'm ninety-nine percent certain that platter was poisoned. Don't worry, at worst you will have a wave of either hope, regret, guilt, anger, or deception. A cigarette should put it out.

—Agent 160

p.s. Someone (else) called about the ad. She said, I have only known adoration and debauchery. Which is saying what? I have only known adoration and pity.

160:
In the future, forward any calls from any women who have known only adoration and debauchery to me. I'll deal with those. Well, between coming off the Plan B and now being poisoned, I'm feeling surprisingly OK. True, there are miniature bats in my peripheral vision, but they tell me they are not vampire bats.

I'm getting tired, agent. Of love, of not love, of drugs, of no drugs. I miss **xxxx** but I'm tired of missing her, and I'm tired of missing something still when I'm not missing her. OK, maybe I am a little poisoned.

During different moments of this report, I became scared and involved, and nervous and giddy, but now I'm just flat. I'm just waiting for the guillotine. Even in Fictional France, I'm not sure a life sentence is worth it. ~K

Agent K:

Who should we invite to the party, er, trial that we're having? We need your supporters there. They should look catastrophic. Something is going to happen. If it doesn't exist, maybe something else will happen.

It is true I miss him, but I miss something else as well. And if I can just miss that other, could I find enough to convince this report to show itself?

It has already bent us all over our heads, our mouths, our feet.

I'm tired too.

Should we look back to the words?

France has a bloody history like we all do.

—Agent 160

p.s. My surveillance team tells me that **xxxx** is not far.

That things are always there.

↙

160:

If she's not far, then **xxxx** may be following the report, a lazy twist. The guy on my corner—a pharmacist of sorts—has assured me that my withdrawal symptoms were psychosomatic (typical)(and a bad business plan at that). He offered a range of alternatives, including one "drug" that was just some crappy toy he must've found in the ditch: a translucent female torso, nude, with a plastic fetus (peach, male). If you shake the torso, the baby rolls around creepily. I included it only for considered inclusion in the tracking device prototype museum.

He offered several alternatives to my little helper, nothing interesting, psychedelics mostly, until the last one: Love Block. Without betraying my extreme inter-est, I bought the toy and asked for the list again "for my boyfriend" (that always turns the radar off).

On the second runthrough, I heard, not Love Block. But Lubbock. You know, the blend of low-quality pot and chewing tobacco in a bigass bag (which actually comes in a bag that says "bigass") popularized in city (same). I have no idea what you're supposed to do with it. I tried running it through the coffee maker, which has slightly improved the smell of my apartment, not that the smell could get worse.

I meant to take a shower after that, but figured I should report this first. Any excuse to not take a shower. So here it is: is it possible we are chasing a typo? Please advise. ~AK

Agent K:

I have never heard of Lubbock, Rilke, or Love Block, but of course that doesn't really tell us if we are chasing a typo since there are many many things, especially in this particular report, that I have never heard of.

The word typo looks like a typo.

In that case, we are free to look for anything we want.

Love cock for instance, rhymes with Love Block.

Did you ever tell me what happened to Plan A?

Is that what started this whole mission?

And who is this pharmacist? Does he deliver cross-country?

Just one plane ticket. One plane ticket.

—Agent 160

Agent K:

Should we meet before the trial? Jot something down? It has been so

long since we've seen each other! I would wear a disguise, but there

is barely a chance you will recognize me.

I sent you some music, pictures of other people, and some stickers.

If you come bring the cat and the pickup.

And drugs 'cause I'm in the Midwest now.

—Agent 160

Agent 160:
Your last message was so cryptic. Actually, it was
not cryptic at all, which is why I've decided it must
be a disguise for a more cryptic message, hidden
within. Like those Russian dolls. If you made Russian
dolls, they wouldn't fit together, and would have
intricate deformities and that's how I'd know they
were yours. I would still love them, of course. Also,
your spelling has gotten strangely sound. Have you
been kidnapped? Is there something you're not
telling me? I won't tell anyone. Everyone has left. It's
just me here. Me and bats. ~AK

AK:

It's true! All of your accusations/observations/drug-induced para-

noia! I have been trying to banish this cloud floating around my

pinkish-purple sky that suddenly decided to say that you don't exist,

that you did, but now you don't. That I have buried you in raw data-

esque, epistolary-esque reportage, leaking out the doggie door. Is it

true?

We should immediately begin shredding. All those tiny tiny stories of tiny tiny moments, with tiny tiny words. It was foolish of me, unprofessional, to become involved. You could have been a contender.

There are mushrooms on my pizza.

Hope all is well,

—Agent 160

Agent 160:
I don't know why you won't take the company jet.
It's unlikely that a freakish mechanical failure will
cause you to make a crash landing for a third time.
Especially if you remember to actually shut all the
doors before takeoff this time. Oh, 160, I wish you
were here, because whatever substance I just
poured into my coffee cup is something that no one
should appreciate alone.
~K

Agent K:

I was recently notified by my dog that the company jet is now dry (no alcohol, no stewardesses).

Operative O did say things would change after my last, um, flight of fancy. He also banned me from all transportation relating to wings and/or objects with less than three wheels.

(Even my talking cloud has left.)

I'm lacing up my department-issued roller skates.

I must say Agent K., you have led me many places, but never astray.

—160

160:
This evening I returned to the Library of Love and

Hate to gather trial evidence. It had been converted into a coffee shop during my house arrest, a coffee shop which serves mainly tea and which does not allow smoking. Which is what? A "No-Coffee" shop?

"Watch my laptop," a boy said. I did, and soon became involved in a competition among patrons for Most Eye Contact with the pornographically hot barista. I complimented her haircut and all of her tattoos and the record she was playing, whatever it was. Clearly, she was in love with me. She glared over every time she poured a shot. Finally, she leaned across the counter, in a way calculated to show the most amount of cleavage. "Your type-writer," she said. "It's kind of loud."

At some point, there was a suggestion that my typewriter and I be forcibly removed (not by my barista, by another barista, who was just jealous), and since showing my agent badge was below my dignity (besides, I look like a tool in that photo), we left (me and the typewriter).

I didn't think about **xxxx** the entire time. Well, unless you count thinking about **xxxx** thinking about me and the pornographically hot barista, which I did think about. Or thinking about **xxxx** being jealous…or thinking about **xxxx** in some kind of elaborate scenario with me, the porno-graphically hot barista and a… Well, anyway, my

point is, has the Love Block—whatever the fuck it
is—worked? And how will we know when it works,
if we keep reporting, keep distracting ourselves?

Hey, where are you, by the way? I checked with
headquarters. Someone suggested we were in love,
and a few people said: hot date. ~AK

❧

Dear Agent K:

Those few people were mistaken. It was the idea of a hot date that

has kept me away. I admit, I went straight for Miss Rose. She said,

you are taller than K, then watched me skate away and somewhere in

there managed to throw an orthopedic shoe at my head.

I fell (gracefully) to the ground. No skating in the library, she said,

her toe pick on my chest. Ice skates, I squeaked. It's about time you

visited, she said.

I let it slip that Miss Plum now runs a coffee shop. She lit a pipe. You

know, Rose said, it is people like you who confuse love for other people. I touched a smoke ring. Agent K. isn't home, I said. She squinted at me and mumbled something about youngsters and trials.

But you are a spring chicken, I told her. She squinted at me again.

I checked the guest list. Pigeon has never been there, then someone clocked me in the hip with a shopping cart full of papers and pliers.

Okay, I admitted to Rose, if it is done, all we can do is say so. She handed me my socks. We convert to a casino at six o'clock.

—160

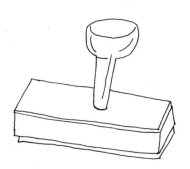

LETTERS NEVER SENT ON PRESUMPTION
OF DEATH, SHAME, OR COWARDICE.
OR GOOD MEASURE.

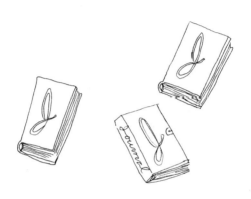

biography

Meghan Austin and Shannon Mullally met while earning their MFAs in Writing at the School of the Art Institute of Chicago. When they agreed to collaborate long-distance on a 3-Day Novel, Austin was living in Portland, Oregon and Mullally was living in Chicago. They both now live in Chicago, where they continue to study and write. This is their first published novel.

the 3-day novel contest

The 3-Day Novel Contest demands that would-be
novelists produce a masterwork of fiction in a mere
72 hours. The contest has run every Labour Day
Weekend since 1977, when a handful of restless
Vancouver writers accepted a challenge to write a
novel over a single long weekend. The call went out,
the gauntlet went down and the 3-Day Novel
Contest was on its way to becoming a cheeky and
uncompromising rebel among literary forms. It has
been called "a fad," "a threat" and a "trial by dead-
line," and it has grown to become a unique contri-
bution to world literary history and a rite of
passage for thousands of writers, from Canada, the
U.S. and beyond.

The 3-Day Novel Contest thanks its friends and
supporters at <www.ABEbooks.com>. Visit
<ABEbooks.com> to search for past winners of the
3-Day Novel Contest, such as *Struck*, by Geoffrey
Bromhead, *Skin*, by Bonnie Bowman, or the very first
winning novel, *Still*, by b.p. nichol.

www.3daynovel.com